WOLF CREEK RANCH

A NOVELLA

BY

PHYLLIS HARRELL

ACKNOWLEDGEMENTS

I want to thank my wonderful husband, Randy, for putting up with me. The long hours of writing and understanding. Babe you are my anchor! I want to thank my best friends Lisa, Marylou and Lissa, girls you rock! But most of all I want to thank all of my family and friends for standing behind me while I was writing this book. I love you all with all of my heart!

PROLOGUE

PART 1

HUNTER AND SUSAN

Susan was just your typical twenty something living the life in Denver. But when she meets the man in her dreams Hunter she is suddenly drawn into the mystical world of wolf shifters. She is knocked off her feet by this purely all male, very hot man. Tall, dark and handsome, with eyes the color of a deep blue sea. He whisks her away to the deep woods of the Rocky Mountains to meet his clan. There he will introduce her to the very sensual and mysterious ways of the wolf.

PROLOGUE

PART 2

SCOTT AND RAY LYNN

Jay Lynn is a Mountain lion shifter who loved having fun. At the local carnival she meets a tall, dark and handsome stranger who knocks her off her feet. But to her surprise Scott is a Wolf shifter. Can they break the barriers of species lore and be together.

PROLOGUE

PART 3

JASON AND LAYLA

Jason was a bachelor and never wanted a mate. Alpha to his pack, his two brothers, Hunter and Scott. But when his two brothers find their mates he thinks just maybe he can find true love. Layla's internal clock is ticking. She needs to find a mate soon. When she meets Jason, a man who knocks her off her feet she must have him. But she is a grisly shifter and he is a wolf shifter. How will they ever find true love and mate.

WARNING SEXUALLY EXPLICIT FOR ADULTS ONLY

CHAPTER 1

A CHANCE MEETING

Susan strummed her fingers on her desk, not even thinking about work, her mind wandering to the recurring dream she had had for the last few weeks. Dreams of a tall, well built, handsome man and of all things, wolves. What is with the wolves! Something deep within her wants to be near them at all times. But the man is always there with the wolves. How strange! She dreams of hot, sweaty, no holds bared sex with him. But the wolves are always nearby, watching over her. Suddenly she is pulled out of the wondering of her mind by her best friend and work partner Catherine. "Hey, Susan, what are you day dreaming about?" I look up at her shyly and say, "Oh, nothing much. How is your day going?" "Boring as always!" We both laugh and she says, "So what is the plan for Friday night? Up for some fun at our favorite bar?" "Sounds good to me. I need some excitement in my boring life!" She gives me a high five and heads off to her office. Flashes of my sexy dream guy goes though my mind. I so wish he was real. Two days later we are at the Broken Oak, a bar in the heart of downtown Denver. We are sitting at a table checking out all the men when "he" walks through the door. The man of my dreams! He stands about 6' 3", has long blonde hair down to the collar of his expensive dress shirt. His body is all muscled and just the sight of him makes my toes curl. But when he looks at me with eyes the color of a deep blue sea I almost melt right there in my scat! I look at Catherine, she has that little "o" on her mouth as she checks him out. I feel a tinge of jealousy knowing she could have him if she wanted him. For you see, she is perfect in every way. Long blonde hair cascades down her back, blue eyes like a summer sky and a body I can only dream of having. I am only 5' 6" and have a soft round body. Don't get me wrong, I have curves in all the right places. But my hips are a little big and my breasts are large and full. I have been told I have a cute heart shaped face and eyes the color of deep emeralds. But still I feel plain next to Catherine. I watch as "he" enters the bar and goes up to order a drink. I feel a tingle run through my body as I watch his magnificent ass in his tight jeans. I feel the flush in my cheeks as he catches me looking at him. I quickly lower my eyes to my hands as I try to get myself under control. Catherine squeals, "Oh, my, gosh, your blushing! Do you have the hots for that gorgeous man at the bar?" My face reddens more when I answer, "I'm not sure but there is something about him. Like I've known him my entire life. I have been dreaming about a man and he looks just like him!" I take another quick glance at the man and those deep blue eyes are looking at me and there is something in those eyes that reminds me of a wild animal. I quickly look back down and then to

5

Catherine. She is looking at me in awe, "Girl, what is going on with you? You look like you could fuck him on the bar!" I pause for a minute to get my faculties back and say, "I don't know, it's like I am drawn to him. When I looked into his eyes all I could think of was wild, carnal sex! I have never felt this way before. Not even with Matt and I loved him with my entire being. Maybe it's just because I miss him so much." Matt was my fiance and had died in a terrible car crash a few months back. The pain still runs deep in my heart. We had been so happy together and were to be married in the Fall. But a drunk driver had taken that all away from me. This had been the first time since the accident I had gone out and now my body was betraying my heart. I wanted this man more than I had ever wanted anyone, even Matt. A deep voice brought me out of my thoughts, "Hello ladies. May I join you this evening?" I looked up at the man and smile, offering him a seat. What the hell is wrong with me! He slipped into the chair next to me and my body became alert to his proximity and I flushed once more. I looked up at him through my lashes and he flashed me a bright, white smile and said, "Hi, my name is Hunter. May I ask your name, beautiful lady?" At first I thought he was talking to Catherine, but his eyes were only for me. I smiled and said, "My name is Susan and this is my friend, Catherine. We are very please to meet you, Hunter." He reached for my hand, lifting it to his lips, kissing ever so lightly saying, "And I am very please to meet you as well. Would you like to dance?" I smiled up at him as I stood, letting him lead me to the dance floor. There was a slow song playing so he took me in his arms and we began to dance. We talked on the dance floor and suddenly he said, "You know, this might sound strange, but I feel as if I have known you my entire life." "Funny you should say that, I was just going to tell you the same thing." I looked up and there was a little sparkle in his eyes as he grinned down at me. He pulled me tight against him and whispered in my ear, "I have been dreaming about you. I cannot believe I have found you. Please come home with me. I want to make love to your beautiful body." A blush crept onto my face as I said, "Yes. I want the same thing. I have been dreaming about you also. In your dreams are there wolves? There are always wolves with us in my dreams." He pulled away from me and said, "You dream of wolves when we are together? Are you sure?" "Yes, I'm sure. There are always two of them. A large black and a smaller brown. Why do you ask?" He looked around the bar for a minute then answered, "We cannot talk here about it. Will you please come to my place so we can talk in private?" I smiled and said, "Lead the way." After I let Catherine know I was leaving with Hunter we left the bar. I had came in Catherine's car so I knew she would get home alright. As we walked to his truck he said, "I have much to tell you about the dreams and once I am done you can decide if you still want to be with me." The ride to his place was quite, we hardly spoke. We arrived at a large ranch outside of town. The sign above the road read "WOLF CREEK RANCH" I turned and asked, "Do you own this ranch?" "Yes, with my two brothers. It used to be our parents but when they died in a accident a few years back we took over." He stopped the truck in front of the house, came around, opened my door and helped me out. The house was enormous. As we walked threw the main doors I took in the front room. There were so many beautiful things and a huge fireplace took up one entire wall. Hunter told me to take a seat on the couch and he would go get us something to drink. He asked, "Do you want a beer or would you prefer wine?" I answered, "Wine would be nice, thank you." A minute after Hunter left to get our drinks two huge men came through the door. One was as tall as Hunter but had black as a raven hair and green eyes. The other man was a few inches shorter with red hair and golden colored eyes, almost like honey. The dark haired man cleared his throat and said, "Excuse me, who are you and what are you doing in our house?" I shook with fear as the man towered over me. I felt like I was frozen in my seat. I couldn't move. Suddenly I hear a growl, look up and there is a wolf crouched behind the man, growling low and menacing. The man turned to the wolf and commanded, "Stop that! Change back now!" I watched as the wolf dropped to his belly bearing his neck to the man. I had no idea why the man was talking about changing, I guess he was telling the wolf to back off. Suddenly the wolf's body began to shimmer. The sound of loud pops and cracks came from the animal. One minute it was an animal, the next a man. Hunter raised from the floor with his eyes on me. He was completely naked. His body solid muscle and his length heavy and hard. He did not try to cover himself, just stood there. The other man said, "Hunter, why did you bring her here?" Hunter replied, "She's mine! We have linked wolf souls." I looked at Hunter and asked, "What are you talking about? What do you mean I'm yours and what is a linked wolf soul?" "I am a wolf shifter and so are my brothers. Jason, the brute, is my oldest brother and our alpha. The man over there is

Scott our youngest brother. I am so sorry you had to see my change like this. I was only trying to protect you. I thought he was going to harm you." I stared at all three men and let out a breath I was holding and said, "So let me get this straight, you guys are werewolves?" "Not exactly, we are men who can shift into wolves. Not the monsters you see on TV. We mean you no harm, you just took us by surprise." Jason stated. Hunter walked over to me and took a seat beside me. He tried to take my hand but I pulled away from him and said, "Don't touch me!" I began to cry. "Please don't cry, Susan. Will you come outside with me so I can speak with you? I promise I won't touch you." "Okay, but then you need to take me home." "If that's what you want after I talk to you then I will." I rose from the couch and followed Hunter outside. The other two stayed inside to give us privacy. We walked to Hunter's truck and he helped me inside. Walking around to the other side, he got in next to me. He said, "Let me start by telling you how truly sorry I am again. My brothers were not expected home until tomorrow. When I saw you in the bar my wolf told me you were our mate. Right now it is mating season for my kind. I have waited many mating seasons for you. When you told me about your dreams I knew you were my destined mate. Please understand, you are it for me. When my wolf saw you it was love and lust at first sight. I had to have you." I sat there staring at him in disbelieve. "Please say something." Hunter said. "What do you want me to say? I'm in shock right now. Please explain to me what is involved with mating. Will I become like you?" He reached for my hand and I aloud him to take it. He answered, "When my kind find their true mate a bond is formed. That is why you were drawn to me. My wolf was calling out to you. That is why when you dreamed of me my wolf was always their. He sought you out and gave you the dreams of me. During mating season the bond pulls us together. I went to the bar looking for you." "So your telling me I am your true mate and there can be no other?" "Yes. Even if you turn me down I will never take another mate." I sat there for a moment then asked, "If I agree to this mating, not saying I will, will I have to become a wolf like you?"

"No, only if you want to. For you to turn it requires me to bite you. This is done during sex. But if you do not want the bite we can still be together. I will not force it on you." I really like the guy but I just couldn't wrap my head around it so I said, "You have given me a lot to think about. I really like you and I think we would be good together. But I would like to go home and think about ever thing you have told me. Can you take me home please?" "Of course. What is your address?" I gave Hunter my address and he put it into his GPS. As we rode in silence I thought about all he had told me. I really liked him a lot but we needed to get to know each other.

CHAPTER 2

WHAT TO DO

After Hunter dropped me off at my place I went to my bedroom, took a shower and sat down on my bed to think. So much was going threw my head it was making me dizzy. It felt like I was dreaming and I would wake up any minute. I got up, went to the kitchen, poured a glass of wine and went back to my bedroom. An hour later I was asleep and dreaming of Hunter. In the dream we were running through the woods, side by side, in wolf form. I was the brown wolf from my earlier dreams. As we ran Hunter nipped at my shoulder playfully urging me to run faster. We arrived at a lake deep in the woods. When we reached the shore we changed back into our human skins. I laid down on the soft grass by the lake and Hunter joined me. Slowly he began kissing down my throat. The heat in me ignited in my core like never before. He licked his way back up to my ear and whispered, "You. Are. Mine! Please let me give you my bite so you will be mine for always!" Susan screamed, "Yes, God yes! I want to be yours till the end of time!" Hunter kiss his way from her ear down to the spot between her neck and shoulder, kissed gently and said, "When we reach our orgasm together I will bite you right here." Susan exclaimed, "I'm so ready for you!" He placed his rock hard shaft at her entrance and slowly he entered. She raised her hips to meet his thrust moaning at how good he felt sliding into her waiting sheath. They began to move together into a fevered pitch. Susan could feel her coming orgasm pushing her closer and closer to release. She took her nails and scored them down his back causing him to pump even harder. Everything tightened inside of her and she screamed, "I'm coming! Please, I need it now!" Hunter licked the spot on her shoulder and she felt his fangs break the skin and she flew apart screaming his name as he came deep within her. Suddenly Susan sat up in her bed looking all around her. She was totally drenched from the orgasm her dream had caused. She thought, "Wow! That was intense!" Slowly she rolled out of bed and headed for the shower. Standing under the warm water she began remember the dream. What she felt in the dream she wanted in real life. She needed to find Hunter and talk to him. She picked up her phone and dialed the number he had given her. Hunter answered on the second ring, "Susan? Are you alright?" "I need to come over and talk to you about another dream I just had. Is it alright if I come?" "Sure, I'll be waiting." Susan quickly got dressed and headed out to Hunter's place. When she arrived he was waiting for her on the porch. He came up, gave her a hug and asked, "What is wrong, you are trembling?" "I had a dream and I need to talk to you about it." "Okay, lets go inside and get out of the cold." Hunter reached for her hand, interlacing their fingers and they walked into the house. He took her over to the sofa and they sat down. "Tell me about this dream and what is bothering you." Susan took a deep breath and said, "It was not a bad dream, but it was strange and erotic. I dreamed you claimed me as your Mate. But the strange thing was, I wanted it so bad I could taste it. Does this mean I also consider you my Mate?" Hunter had the most beautiful smile on his face as he said, "Yes, I had the same dream. My wolf was there with you in the dream claiming you as his. Now all that is left is for me to claim you in real life. Susan, will you become my Mate? Please do me the honor of becoming mine." Susan did not hesitate when she gave her answer, "Yes! I want to be yours for always!" Hunter took her in his arms and began kissing her passionately. He lifted her into his arms and carried her to his bedroom, placing her on his bed. Without breaking their kiss he began removing her clothes. He pushed her shirt up, exposing her breasts. She had no bra on and his glaze ran down her chest to the hard peaks of her nipples. He broke the kiss, lifting her up to remove the shirt the rest of the way. Once he had her free of the shirt he began to kiss and lick down her throat till he reached the valley between her breasts. He looked up at Susan and said, "Mate, you taste good enough to eat and I am going to taste every part of your body!" Susan shivered at his words and moaned. Hunter took the hard nub of her left breast into his mouth and sucked eagerly, licking around the tip. Then he went to her right and gave the same pleasure and attention to it. By then Susan was moaning louder and rubbing her pelvis against his rock hard shaft. Moaning she said, "More, I need more!" He released the nub of her right breast and slowly began to lick down her body stopping at her belly button. Swirling his tongue into the little dip he continued down to the top of her mound. Susan wiggled beneath him as his fingers found her acing, drenched opening. As he slip a finger in, he latched onto her clit, sucking gently. Susan thrust her hips up locking them around his head as her orgasm took her over the edge screaming his name. Hunter gave her long hard lick from opening to clit then started his trail back up her body until he reached her mouth. He plunged his tongue in and she could taste herself. He broke his kiss saying, "God, you are so beautiful and you taste like heaven! Are you ready for me? My Mate." "Yes! Claim me now and make me yours forever!!" Hunter placed his hard shaft at her opening and slowly, inch by inch slid into her warm heat. It felt like home. His wolf howled, "Mine! Mine! Mine!" Hunter raised up on his elbows staring down into Susan's heated glaze. God she was beautiful and now she would be his. He began to pump into her and she raised her legs, wrapping them around his waist meeting his every thrust. Hunter could feel her coming orgasm as her tight sheath squeezed his cock. He started to pump faster as he felt his balls tighten with his coming release. He growled low in his throat, his wolf so close to the surface and said, "I am going to give you my bite now and make you mine forever!" Licking down her throat to where her neck met her shoulder he felt his fangs extend as he breached her skin. Susan screamed and froze as her orgasm took her, causing Hunter to pound into her chasing his own release. His hot seed flowed into her waiting channel, filling her to the brim. He collapsed on top of her panting wildly. Licking his mark he said, "Mate, how do you feel? Did I hurt you?" "No, I feel wonderful! Oh Hunter, I am so happy! I love you!" "As I love you, Mate!" Hunter slowly withdrew from her, rolled to his side and took her into his arms. Soon they feel into a sound sleep.

CHAPTER 3

THE CHANGE

The following morning Susan awoke, stretching her sore muscles. Amazed at how well she felt, other than a strange itching to her skin. She rolled over and found blazing blue eyes smiling at her. "Good morning, my beautiful Mate. How did you sleep?" Susan reached up feeling the mating mark on her shoulder and smile. "Like a woman in love and happily mated!" Hunter smiled down at her rubbing his hard steel against her belly. "Are you ready for round two my beauty?" She smiled up at him, grabbed his head, pulling him down for a kiss, letting him know just how ready she was. A few hours later they were up and dressed. Hunter was in the kitchen making them breakfast as she poured them coffee. She sat the cups down on the breakfast bar and said, "Baby, I need to ask you a question." "Sure, what is it?" "In my dream I am also a wolf, will I become like you?" "Yes, my bite gave you our bond, soon you will be running with me as your wolf." "How will I know when it is going to happen?" "At first you skin will begin to itch. This is your wolf letting you know she wants out. A few days later you will change." "I was itching this morning, so that means in a few days I will become my wolf?" "Yes, I can hardly wait to see your beautiful she-wolf!" Susan smiled up at him saying, "Me too! I cannot wait to run wild with you at my side. I love you so much Hunter!" "I love you too, my beautiful Mate!" After breakfast Hunter took her around the ranch showing her all the beauty of his land. Around lunch time they return to the house and found both his brothers there waiting for them. "Good morning guys. How are you today?" Hunter asked. Both his brothers looked at him and said together, "What the hell is going on? Why is she here?" Hunter squared his shoulders and stated, "She is my Mate. I marked her last night and she will be turning soon." Hunter's brother and Alpha Jason asked, "What do you mean mate, you hardly know this woman." Hunter could feel the Alpha's timber in his brother's tone but he was not going to bow down this time. Susan was his Mate and he would fight even his

Alpha to keep her. "Jason, it is already done. She is mine and I will not allow you to harm her in any way." "Harm her? Are you kidding? I would never harm a female. I just don't understand how you could claim a woman you barely know." "Some day, when you meet your mate, you will understand brother. She is everything to me and I am nothing without her." "Okay, I will not interfere in you mating. As you said, she is the one and you should know if your wolf allowed you to claim her." Scott, Hunter's younger brother, who had been quit the whole time came up to Hunter, clapped him on the back and said, "Congratulations, brother. I only hope I will find my mate soon." Scott took Susan in a bear hug saying, "Welcome to the family, my brother's Mate!" Susan grinned and said, "Thank you, Scott. I'm so happy to be here." A few minutes later the brother's left to take care of the horses. Susan placed her arms around Hunter's waist and said, "What was with Jason? And why did I feel like cowering when he first spoke to you?" "Jason is our Alpha. Your wolf felt his authority when he spoke. He can be a little overpowering when he goes all Alpha on us. But inside he's just a big pussy cat." Susan laughed and said, "So, my wolf is close to coming out now? Is that why she acted the way she did with you Alpha?" "Yes, you should be changing soon." "Will it hunt Hunter?" "It will the first time, but I will be there with you the whole time." "Good, I don't know if I could do it alone. I'm so scared!" "There is nothing to be scared of, it will be over quickly and then we will run the woods free to be ourselves." "I love you so much, Hunter. I'm so glad you chose me as your Mate!" "I knew you were mine the first time I laid eyes on you in the bar. My wolf kept yelling, "MINE" telling me your were ours." After lunch Hunter ask Susan if she wanted to go horseback riding. She answered, "I haven't been in a very long time. I don't know if I could still do it." "Honey, it's like riding a bike. It just takes a little time to get use to doing it again." "Sounds good to me. Let's go." She grabbed Hunter's hand, pulling him toward the door. Soon they were out riding through a beautiful trail in the woods. Hunter had told her he wanted to take her somewhere special. As they rode throw the woods they came upon a beautiful lake with a waterfall. Susan exclaimed, "Oh Hunter, it is so beautiful here! My God, that waterfall is breathtaking." "I knew you would love it. Want to go for a swim?" "We didn't bring any swimming suits." "So." Hunter said with a glint in his eyes. Susan laughed and ran to the edge of the water with Hunter right on her heels. He was ripping his clothes off as he ran. Splashing into the water he said, "What are you waiting for? Show me your beautiful body!" Susan stripped out of her clothing, giggling the whole time and ran into the water. As she reached Hunter she splashed him. He dropped beneath the water and she could not see him. Suddenly she felt a tug on her legs and she went under.

A few seconds later she came up gasping for air. Hunter had her in a tight embrace. She smacked him on the shoulder, playfully and said, "Silly man, are you trying to drown me?" Hunter laughed, "That's what you get for splashing me!" He then took her mouth in a slow passionate kiss. Susan wrapped her legs around his waist and said, "Make love to me, my Mate." Hunter carried her from the lake and laid her down on the soft grass. Hovering over her he said, "You are so beautiful! I love your curves. They fit perfectly to my body." Hunter took her left nipple into his mouth and sucked gently. Susan moan at the feel of it. She looked up at him and said, "I need you inside of me now! Please, I cannot wait another moment." Hunter placed his rock hard shaft at her entrance and slowly slid into her heat. Soon he was pounding hard into her slick, tight sheath. Susan was moaning at the feel of his cock sliding in and out of her. Suddenly Hunter flipped her over onto her hands and knees, entering her from behind, setting a growling pace. Suddenly Susan felt a pain in her gums as her fangs extended. Her fingers dug into the soft earth as long black claws extended. Just as they both reached their release a howl escaped her lips. She rolled away from Hunter, loud popping noises coming from within her body. She looked down and saw paws where her feet should have been. Her hearing and sense of smell was greatly increased. She turned, in her wolf form and looked at Hunter. He had the hugest smile on his face.

"God, your beautiful, my Mate!" Susan watched as Hunter's body began to shimmer and then the beautiful black wolf of her dreams stood before her. Slowly she came up to him and sniffed his neck. God he smelled good. Suddenly she heard his voice in her head. "How do you feel, my beautiful she-wolf?" She answered back within her mind, "Wow! This is amazing! But how am I hearing you within my mind?" "It is our bond. It allows us to talk to each over. Are you up to a run through the woods?" Susan smiled a wolfish smile and yelled, "Catch me if you can!" Then she took off like the wind with Hunter right on her heels.

35

FROM THE AUTHOR

I hope you enjoyed Susan and Hunter's story. Please continue reading below for Scott's story.

Chapter 4

Scott

Scott watched as Susan and Hunter ran off into the woods in their wolf forms. God how he wished he would be so lucky. But he had yet to find his destined ate. His Alpha and brother, Jason had assured him hat he would find her soon but there was only a few weeks left in mating season and if he did not find her he would have to wait a whole year before he could search again. Scott went t his room to get ready for the search again tonight. He would go into the city of Colorado Springs in search of her this evening. There was a carnival in town tonight and hopefully he would find his mate.

Shortly after 7pm he arrived at the carnival. There was hundreds of people roaming around enjoying the attractions. Scott's friend Josh was manning a food both nearby so he went over to say hello. "Hey Josh, how's it going?" "Not to bad. I have had quite a few customers already. What ya doing here? Looking for that special lady?" Scott answered with a huff, "Yep. But it is so damn hard. I only have a few weeks left to find her, then I will have to wait a whole norther year!" "Man that sucks. I am so glad I found Amber last mating season. But I know you will find that someone special soon. I just know it!" Scott gave a small smile and said, "I hope your right man, this is driving me crazy. Seeing Hunter so happy with his mate is making me want the same thing." They talked for a few minutes more and Scott said goodbye and went out into the crowd.

CHAPTER 5

RAY LYNN

It was Saturday night and Ray Lynn was getting ready to go to the carnival in town. Her friend Stacie was getting ready right alone side of her. Ray Lynn sighed and said to her friend, "Do you think we will find our mates tonight? I am so ready to settle down!" Stacie laughed and answered, "I sure hope so. I am so tired of the dating scene! Hopefully we will find a couple of nice cats to settle down with tonight." They both laughed. The mountain lion in her rubbed near the surface just at the thought of a mate. The thought of having a cub in her belly pulled strongly at her. She had to find her mate tonight! Soon they arrived at the carnival and started looking around. There was hundreds of people milling about and the noise hurt her sensitive ears. They grabbed an ice cream from a nearby vendor and took a seat on a bench. Ray Lynn watched as couples walked by, hand in hand. How she wished that was her. Suddenly she caught sight of a gorgeous man at one of the vendor stands talking to the man inside. He was six feet of pure muscle. She watched as his muscles bulged in his broad back as he spoke with the vendor. She let her eyes travel down the length of him, settling on his tight ass. She felt her cat roar "MINE" Slowly the man turned to leave and she caught sight of his face. He had beautiful blue eyes, a straight narrow nose and perfect plump lips for kissing. Her lion began scratching at her insides wanting out hissing over and over "Mine. Mine. Mine!" Ray Lynn let her sense of smell range out, testing the air for his scent. When it finally hit her she cringed back. This was no cat shifter, all she could smell was wolf. What the hell. Why was her cat so taken by a wolf shifter? They were different species for god sake. But her lion would not shut up. She turned to look at Stacie who had a "What the fuck?" look on her face. Ray Lynn blushed and said, "I know, my cat is dying to come out and play with the wolf. Does that make any sense to you? We are not even the same species!" Stacie just shrugged her shoulders and said, "Who knows? But when the animal in us chooses we have no control over the urge to mate." Ray Lynn just shook her head. How was this possible? How could she want the wolf so much. She looked up from her thoughts and there he was staring her dead in the eyes.

CHAPTER 6

SCOTT

I'm standing there minding my own business talking to Josh when it hits me. The feeling of being watched. My Wolf's hackles rose and he sniffed the air. He smelled cat lingering in the air, heavy with arousal. But why was wolf so interested in the scent of a mountain lioness? He turned around slowly and caught the sight of a female that stopped his breath. She was beautiful! Long blonde hair cascaded down her shoulders and onto her back. She had a heart shaped face with beautiful green eyes the color of emeralds, a button nose and plump red lips made for kissing. Her body was round and soft with breasts made to fit in his hands. His wolf rose to the surface and roared, "MINE! MATE!" But how could this be? He was a wolf and she was a mountain lion it could never work! But the pull was to strong to ignore. Slowly he made his way over to her until he was standing right in front of her. She looked up at him with those beautiful green eyes and he was lost. She dropped her eyes to her hands and blushed the most beautiful rose color he had ever seen. After a few seconds he finally got up the nerve to speak. "Hello, my name is Scott. My I ask what you beautiful ladies names are?" Right away the other woman spoke up, "My name is Stacie and this is my friend Ray Lynn. We are pleased to meet you, Scott." He thought to himself, Ray Lynn, what a beautiful name. She looked up at him and smiled saying, "We are very pleased to meet you, Scott." His heart soared at hearing his name on those beautiful lips. "Would you ladies like to accompany me around the carnival?" The girls both looked at each other and giggled. Then Ray Lynn replied, "We would love to Scott, lead the way.

CHAPTER 7

RAY LYNN

Ray Lynn could not believe the man was asking them to join him. God he was hot! All should could think about was getting him alone. But she could not do that to her friend so they followed him out into the crowd. Soon they were standing in line in front of the Ferris Wheel. Stacie had excused herself to go to the ladies room and said she would meet up with them after the ride was done. As the wheel came to a stop and the couple on board got off Scott held out his hand to her. As soon as their fingers touched a spark went straight to her core. Suddenly she found herself being very shy. He helped her up into the seat and joined her. The carny checked to make sure they were locked in and then the wheel began to lift. Scott had his arm behind her and she felt the bulging muscles of his bicep and forearm. Her whole body was tingling at his closeness. Suddenly she caught a whiff of his arousal. Damn he was into her as much as she was into him. He squeezed her shoulder and she thought she would melt. She turned to look into the depths of his blue eyes and saw the animal rise up in him. Her lioness purred from close to the surface. As they reached the top and stopped to take on another couple below Scott ran his fingers over her lips and said, "I would love to kiss you right now. Am I being to forward?" She smiled and said, "No. I want it as much as you do." Taking her chin in his big hand he turned her to him and took her lips in a soft kiss. Her lioness clawed at her insides wanting more. The tip of his tongue brushed her lips asking for entrance. She opened her mouth slightly and he slipped in. God he tasted good! He deepened the kiss and there tongues clashed. She couldn't get enough of him. The wheel jerked beginning their descent, breaking them apart. Ray Lynn panted needing him back in her mouth. The rumble coming from Scott's chest told her he wanted the same. As they lowered to the ground he ask, "If I'm not being to bold, will you come home with me?" She smiled up at him without hesitation and answered, "Sure." Once they were off the ride they looked for Stacie. She spotted her talking to a tall good looking man. She ask Scott to wait there for her, she would be right back. Running over to Stacie she pulled her aside. "Hey, do you mind if I leave with Scott? I don't want to go off if you need me." Stacie smiled and said, "No problem. I think I'm going to hang around for a bit to get to know Sam better." She pointed to the man she had been talking to. They both giggled, said their goodbyes and would catch each other up later. She walked over to Scott, took his hand and said, "I'm ready if you are." He smiled and led her away from the carnival.

CHAPTER 8

SCOTT

Scott could not believe his luck. The beautiful Ray Lynn was going back to the ranch with him. His heart hammered in his chest. He opened the passenger door of his truck and helped her into the seat then went around and got in, started up the truck and headed for the ranch. He reached over and took her hand in his, raised it to his lips and kissed. RayLynn gave him a glorious smile. He thought to himself, "Could she be the one he has been searching for all these years?" His wolf raised up in him and roared, "Mine! Ours! Mate!" But how could it be? He was a wolf and she was a lioness, could the two species mix? If they were not compatible he did not know what he would do. But right now all he could think about was sinking into her warm heat and making love to her all night. To hell with compatibility, he would find out later. He wanted her, wolf wanted her and nothing was going to stand in their way. Fifteen minutes later they arrived at the ranch. He left the driver's side, going around to open the door for her. Reaching inside he pulled her into his arms and carried her into the house. She smacked him on the shoulder saying, "Put me down silly, I can walk!" He gave a little chuckle and said, "I love the feel of you in my arms! I may never put you down!" He carried her down the hall to his bedroom. He shared the house with his two brothers but his brother Hunter had found his mate and was building her a house. Soon they would be out. Right now he had the house and her all to himself. He kicked his bedroom door open, entered, then kicked it shut heading for his large bed. He laid her down on the bed, leaning over her, feeling her soft body beneath him. It was like heaven, like home. He slowly lowered himself to her lips and took them passionately. She reached around him, scoring her nails in his back. God she was hot! He reached for her T-shirt, pushing up to expose her breast. She had nothing on underneath. He broke the kiss looking down at her exposed breast. The nipples were large and pointed. He bent down taking one into his mouth sucking gently. A moan escaped from her lips.

She ground her hips into his already swollen cock causing him to make a moan of his own. While still sucking on her taunt nipple he reached down and unbuttoned her shorts sliding them down along with her panties. He could smell her arousal and it was driving him crazy. He had to have a taste. He released her nipple and licked down her chest until he reached her navel, running his tongue around the little opening. She panted out, "More, please!" He licked down farther until he reached the top of her mound. She was total hairless. This turned him on even more. He slide his tongue across her clit and she jerked in surprise. He lifted her legs so they were over his shoulders, pulling her pussy lips apart he dove in. Her sweetness assaulted his tongue sending him into a frenzy. He licked her slick wet hole and back up to her clit, taking the small bundle of nerves into his mouth and sucked hard. She bucked up into his mouth and screamed as she came hard. He enter a finger into her hot wetness and felt how tight she was. He need to make her ready for his large cock so he into another finger. Slowly he finger fucked her while he continued to suck on her little bundle. Soon she was cumming again screaming his name. He raised up and removed all of his clothing. He watched as her hooded eyes zoned in on his enormous cock. She licked her lips and said, "I want to taste that beautiful thing!" She sat up, pushing him back on the bed and straddled him. She reached for his cock, stroking it up and down. He groaned and pumped his cock into her fist. Slowly she leaned over and placed her lips on his tip, licking circles around it. Her mouth slide down the length of him, taking his whole cock into her hot little mouth. Coming back up she ran the tip of her tongue up the hard vain underneath and almost made him shot his load in her mouth. Getting himself under control he reached for her, turning her around to face him and lifted her onto his hard cock. She was warm and wet, her juices running down his cock coating it. Inch by inch he slid into her tight sheath until he was balls deep. He held still while she adjusted to his size. A moan escaped from her lips and she said, "Oh God, you feel so good. I need you to move!" He pulled out slowly letting her savor the feel of him then plunged back in rolling his hips. She screamed as she came hard around his cock yelling his name. In a blink of an eye he had her underneath him pounding hard into her. He felt his on release coming as his ball tighten close to his body. Panting out at her neck he said, "I want you as my mate always. I want to put my mark on you, I want to place my seed in you and watch your belly grow with my child. Please say yes." Ray Lynn moaned and said, "Yes, Mate, I want you as my mate! Take me! Mark me! Make me yours!!" Scott felt his fangs extend and he clamped down on her shoulder sending them both over the edge. He was floating on a cloud. This woman had agreed to be his and now she was. His wolf howled over and over, "Mate. Mine.

Ours!

FROM THE AUTHOR

I hope you enjoyed Scott and Ray Lynn's story. Please continue below for the final chapter of Wolf Creek Ranch. Jason's story

CHAPTER 9

JASON

Damn, my brothers are driving me crazy! All this talk of mates. My brother Hunter with his little human/wolf mate. Scott with his mountain lioness. What was the deal with that? I did not think we could mate outside of our own species. But there they were happy, in love and expecting a child. Hunter's mate, Susan had given birth last month to a male cub and now who knows what this new child would be. He shivered at the thought. Being Alpha of this growing pack was starting to put a strain on him. All the happiness around him was making him sick. He had to get away for a little while. He had heard there was going to be a big sale of horses up in Saddle

Creek next month. Maybe this would be a way for him

to get away from all the lovey dovey going on. He hated

the thought of having a mate. He had always been a

bachelor and planned on keeping it that way. He didn't

need a woman tying him down. He got up from the

breakfast table, telling everyone he was headed out to

check on the horses and would be back later. It was time

to let his wolf out. He had been clawing at him for the

last week wanting out. He went to the barn, undressed,

dropped to all fours and called his wolf forward. He felt

as the bones popped and reshaped and claws replaced

fingers. Soon his human body was replaced with that of

a large gray wolf. Bounding forward he ran toward the

woods. Soon he reached his favorite place in the woods. A large meadow covered in wildflowers. Here he could run and chase rabbits to his hearts content. After about an hour he lowered himself to the soft grass and placed his head in his paws. This was the life he had always wanted. No ties to a female, no cubs to chase after, just his carefree bachelor ways.

CHAPTER 10

LAYLA

Layla was a grisly bear shifter in her prime. She needed a mate badly. But so far over the years she had been unlucky in love. She needed to find a mate soon or she would end up an old maid with no cubs. Her maternal insistent was high. There was only a few more weeks to mating season then she would have to wait another year to find her mate. She dreamed of love and happiness with a mate and did not want to take someone just to please her bear. Her bear huffed. She was so ready to mate. But to hell with her, she would not take a mate until she knew he loved her. Her alpha, John had suggested she try to seek out her mate in another town and stop looking in Saddle Creek but she just couldn't make herself leave. She felt like she would find her destined mate here. Reaching the edge of the woods she shifted back into her human skin and picked up the bundle of clothes she had left by a tree. Once she was dressed she headed back into town. John greeted her at the entrance to their compound. A large ranch style home located right outside of town. "Layla, where have you been? I have been looking all over for you." "I went for a run in the woods. Why? What do you need?" "We have buyers coming in this afternoon to look at the horses and I need you to meet them in town and bring them out here." "Sure, no problem. When are they arriving?" "Around 1pm. I asked that they meet you at the Double Oak Tavern." Layla looked at her watch. It was already 11:30 so she best be on her way. She said goodbye to her alpha and headed into town. She took the ranch's large van to bring the buyers back. About fifteen minutes later she arrived at her destination. There was already a few buyers milling around the tavern have a beer. There was five in all, but her alpha had told her there would be six. Looking around she watched as a tall, very well muscled man entered the tavern. He had hair the color of corn silk that hung to his shoulders. His face was handsome in a rugged kind of way. With high cheek bones, a chiseled nose and the most stunning brown eyes she had ever seen. They had fakes of gold in them making them sparkle. Her bear rose up on it's hind legs inside of her and sniffed the air and roared, "MATE!" She cleared her head and walked over to the stranger and ask, "Hi, are you here for the horse sale?" He smiled down at her with those sparkling eyes, taking her breath away and said, "Yes. My name is Jason, I am from the Wolf Creek Ranch. May I ask your name, pretty lady?" She gave him a quick smile and said, "My name is Layla. I am with Shady Oaks Ranch and will be taking you back to view our horses." Jason smiled at her and said, "Lead the way."

CHAPTER 11

JASON

God she was beautiful. A face that would break any man's heart. Eyes the color of honey and hair the color of wheat. Her body was to die for. Curves in all the right places with beautiful full breast a man could get lost in. She had a narrow waist and hips that flared out just like he liked them. He could see himself grabbing those hips and pounding into her beautiful body. His wolf howled in agreement. What the fuck? His wolf had never taken this much interest in a woman before. He took a deep breath, taking in her scent. Instantly he smelled bear, but also sunshine after a good rain. But also something else right below the surface. Honey! She smelled like the sweetest honey. He shook his head to clear his senses, his wolf prowling right below his skin. Wolf was yelling, "Mine! Ours! Mate!" No way. That was impossible. He never wanted a mate. He followed her out to a van and everyone got in. Soon they were on their way. Within the confounds of the van her honey scent accosted his nose. God she smell so sweet. All he could think about was getting a taste. After a short ride they arrived at Shady Oaks Ranch. A large man came out of the house to greet them. Could this be her mate? His wolf so wanted to find out. He wanted to claim this woman as his own. What the fuck wolf? I do not and never will want to claim any woman! His wolf growled at him and said, "OURS! MATE!" Damn, his wolf was on the warpath! Layla led everyone over to the man and said, "Gentlemen, this is my brother John. He will be showing our horses to you." With that she turned and walked into the house. Jason's wolf howled wanting her to come back. John instructed everyone to follow him and we all headed to a large paddock in the back of the house.

CHAPTER 12

LAYLA

Layla closed the door behind her as the men left to look at the horses. Her heart was pounding in her chest. In the van coming up she had scented humans with one exception. She scented a wolf shifter. Could it be Jason? He seamed so much bigger than the other men. He had the build of a shifter and the looks to go with that body. But if he was the wolf it would never work out with them. How could it? She was a bear. Species do not mix do they? All she knew was she wanted him and was going to find out before he left. Dinner had been arranged for the group of men. So she had a little time to research. She went to her room and fired up her computer. There was a special place in the deep web where shifters went to find out about each other. She entered her password, logging into the site. She went to the search bar and typed in "Inter species mating" and waited. Soon information began to appear. To her surprise it was possible. There was many stories of couples of different species happily mate. Her heart ached. Could it be possible. Could Jason be her fated mate? She had felt the pull to him and her bear had partially drooled at the sight of him. She had to get him alone and talk to him before he left. She would wait until dinner then ask if he would like to go for a walk with her. If he turned her down it would break her heart.

An hour later the men returned from checking out the horses and were in deep conversation. From the sound of it there was a bidding war going on. She greeted them and ask them to follow her into the dining room. Once Jason was seated she quickly took the seat next to him. Their cook, Thomas brought out a large pot roast and placed it in the center of the table. There was potatoes, carrots and onions all around the roast. God it smell good. There was large baskets of yeast rolls on ether side of the table. There was wine and beer available along with water. John said grace then told everyone to dig in. Layla took a small portion of each item and placed them on her plate. Jason looked at her and asked, Is that all your eating? You eat like a bird." She smiled at him and said, "I'm not really hungry right now. I had a big lunch." He shrugged his shoulders and began to eat. How was she going to talk to him? He didn't seem interested in her at all.

CHAPTER 13

JASON

God she smelled good. Sitting right next to her made his wolf sit up and howl. He had watched her take very small portion of the meal onto her plate. His wolf yelled, "Feed her!" What the hell! He took a deep breath and it hit him like a brick wall. Underneath the smell of delicious honey was bear. Damn, she was a bear shifter. But his wolf did not care. He kept up with the "MINE" stuff. Was it possible she was his fated mate? His wolf shook his head vigorously. But he tramped the thought down. He did not want a mate, fated or not. No sir, mated life was not for him. He enjoyed his freedom to much to be tied down to a woman. But his wolf disagreed with him. He wanted more, he wanted the whole thing. A mate, love, cubs. Just when he shook the thought from his head he felt her small hand on his and bachelorhood flew out the window. He felt the electricity run straight to his cock and it hardened at her touch. He shifted a little in his chair as his erection became uncomfortable. He looked into her eyes and there was a knowing twinkle there. She spoke in a hushed voice, "Would you like to go for a walk with me?" Hell ya, he couldn't wait to take her in his arms and kiss her senseless. He smiled and said, "Sure, that sounds nice." They both stood up from the table and excused themselves. John gave his sister a questioning

look and she just smiled at him. Once outside she said,
"I would like to show you my prized possession. Would
you like to meet him? He is such a beautiful animal."
"That would be great, lead the way." Once the reached
the barn she lead him inside. Walking past a few stalls
they stopped at the fourth one back. There in the stall
stood the most beautiful horse he had ever seen. A black
as pitch stallion. The horse clawed at the ground with
his hoof. Shook his head and reared back. Layla cooed
at him with a quite voice and he lowered his head. She
reached up, rubbing him between his eyes. "His name is
Satan. I raised him from a colt. What do you think of
him?" "God he's beautiful. But why did you name him
Satan?" She smiled and said, "As you probably know by

now I am a bear shifter. I know you are a wolf, I scented you when we were in the van. When I was very young, still a cub, my mother told me stories of a beautiful black stallion she admired from afar. No one could get near the animal. Everyone called him Satin. One day my mother was out hunting in bear form when she cane upon the horse. He had caught himself in a barbed wire fence. When the horse saw her he was so scared he tried to pull free of the wire causing it to dig into his hide more. My mother quickly shifted into her human skin and cooed at the horse trying to get him to calm down. To her surprise he bowed his head to her. She walked up to him and gently untangled him from the wire. Once free he whinnied at her, nudging her neck. From that day forward he allowed only her to come near him. My

Satin is his son. Like his father with my mother, he will

not let anyone near him but me." "He looks very

spirited. Are you able to ride him?" "Yes, but only

bareback he will not allow a saddle on his back." They

stayed there for a few minutes more admiring to

beautiful animal and then left. Layla took him down a

winding path into the woods. "I have someplace I would

like to show you." Jason smiled and said, "Great. Lead

the way." She took his hand, leading him out of the

barn. Slowly they walked off toward the woods. Soon

they reached a small lake with a waterfall cascading

down into it. "This is my most favorite place in the

world." She said. Jason looked toward the waterfall and

said, "Wow! What a beautiful site, I can see why you love it so much." She lead him over to the edge of the water and asked, "Would you like to go for a swim?" He smiled down at her and began removing his shirt. He watched as she removed her clothing, stripping down to just her bra and panties. God, her body was perfect. Curves in all the right places. He watched as she reached behind and unclasp her bra, letting it fall away. Her breast were round and firm with hard peaks of pink flesh. She looked up at him and he could see lust in her eyes. Quickly he removed his pants and boxers. His cock sprang free and was already hard for her. She licked her lips as her eyes perused his hard muscular body until those beautiful eyes reached his cock. Slowly she approached him, her hips swaying. She reached up, touching his face and said, "I want you so bad! Please, I need you now!" Jason pulled her to his lips, kissing her passionately. She felt so wonderful in his arms. Wolf was screaming his pleasure at the feel of her. "Take her! She is ours! Mate! Mate! Mate!" He tried to quite the wolf as he deepened the kiss, pressing his tongue asking for entrance. She opened her mouth and he plunged in. Tasting the most exquisite thing he had in his life. She tasted of sunlight, a spring breeze and honey. He licked and in entwined his tongue with her's. A moan escaped her lips and his cock hardened more, to the point of pain. He needed inside of her so bad. But he had to take it slow, prepare her for him. He lowered her to the ground slowly as he continued to kiss her. Placing her on the soft grass he broke the kiss saying, "You are so beautiful! I want you so badly. Do you want me as bad as I want you?" She looked up at him with a smile and answered, "Oh Jason, I have wanted you from the first time I saw you. Please, I need you so badly!" He took her lips again in a hard, passionate kiss. His hands roaming her body. He squeezed her right nipple between his thumb and forefinger, causing her to thrust her chest into his hand and she moaned. He left her lips, kissing down her throat to her breast. Slowly her took the hard nub into his mouth and sucked gently. Her hands went into his hair, pulling softly, letting him know that she was enjoying his lips on her breast. After a few licks around the nipple, he went for her other. Sucking a little harder he caused her body to arch up into his. He could feel the heat of mound against his cock. He left her breast and licked all the way down to that heat. Reaching her womanhood he blew his hot breath on her clit, causing her to shudder and moan. As he licked her waiting bundle of nerves she screamed his name as her orgasm took her. He slipped two fingers into her hot sheath, feeling them tighten around him with her orgasm. "God, you are so hot and wet for me! I cannot wait until I feel your pussy around my cock!" "Take me now! I need to feel you deep inside of me!" He removed his fingers and mouth from her sex. Slowly he pulled himself up her body until his throbbing cock was at her entrance. He took her lips as he slowly began to slide inside. He moaned, "So tight, so hot. You feel so good. You. Are. Mine!" Layla moaned at the feel of him sliding into her. She had never wanted a male more than she did now. He felt right, felt like home. At that very moment her bear growled, "MATE!" her heart pounding with her coming release. She looked into Jason's eyes seeing something she had never seen before. Not just lust, but love. He was hers as much as she was his. As he filled her, making every nerve ending in her body sing she said, "I want you Jason, forever! Take me and mate me now." He smiled down at her saying, "I thought you would never ask!" He lower his mouth to her neck, kissing gently. He felt his cock grow even harder with his coming release. He licked the spot between her neck and shoulders. Feeling his fangs extend, he bit down. Layla screamed as her pussy clenched, milking his orgasm from him. He buried himself deep within her hot channel, releasing his hot cum, filling her completely with his seed. They laid there, holding each other as they came down from their high. Jason raised up, still buried deep within her, feeling his cock growing again and said, "My mate, are you ready for round two?" She smiled up at him, "Yes!" He slowly pulled back and entered her again as she moaned loudly. A few hours later they returned to her family to announce their mating. Everyone was so have for the couple. Jason could not wait to get back to the ranch and let his brothers know he was mated and their pack was complete. He took Layla's hand in his and said, "Let's go home, Mate."

FROM THE ARTHOR

I hope you have enjoyed the boy's stories. Stay tuned for more stories of hot, steamy, shifter romance.

Please leave your feedback and let me know what you thought of story.

Made in the USA
Charleston, SC
25 February 2016